The
Three Little
Pirates

Ahoy there!

Look out for more storybooks by
Georgie Adams and Emily Bolam…

The Three Little Princesses
The Three Little Witches

The Three Little Pirates

Georgie Adams and Emily Bolam

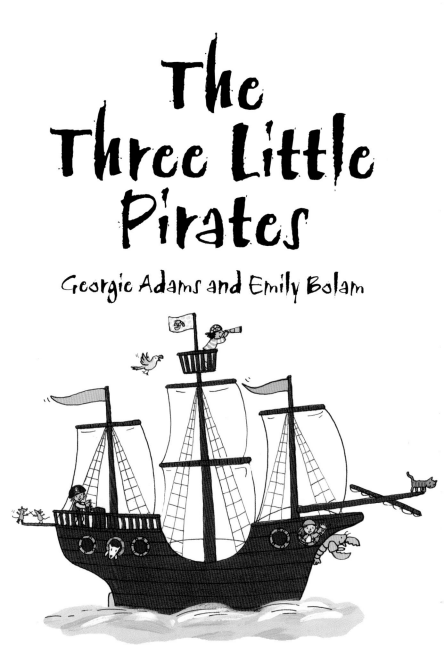

Orion
Children's Books

First published in Great Britain in 2006
by Orion Children's Books
This edition first published in Great Britain in 2010
by Orion Children's Books
a division of the Orion Publishing Group Ltd
Orion House
5 Upper St Martin's Lane
London WC2H 9EA
An Hachette UK Company

1 3 5 7 9 10 8 6 4 2

A catalogue record for this book is available from the British Library.

ISBN 978 1 4440 0084 9

Printed in China

The Orion Publishing Group's policy is to use papers that are natural,
renewable and recyclable products made from wood grown in sustainable forests.
The logging and manufacturing processes are expected to conform
to the environmental regulations of the country of origin.

www.orionbooks.co.uk

For Tom – a very special pirate!
With love,
G.A.

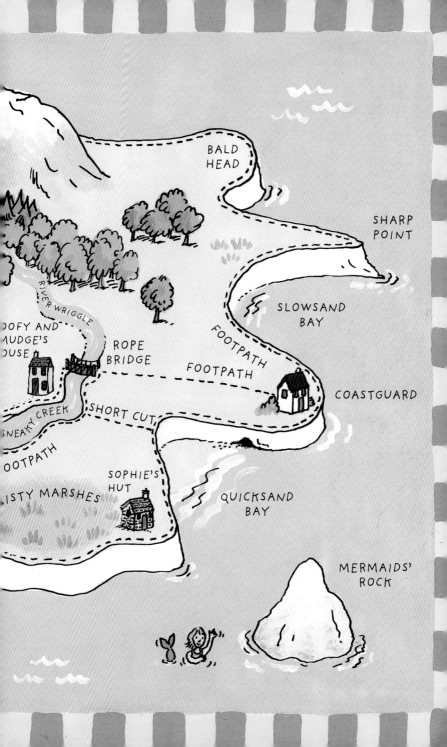

Contents

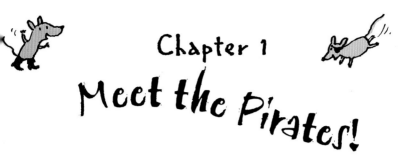

Chapter 1
Meet the Pirates!

Ahoy there! Let's meet the three little pirates:

This is Trixy and her dog, Mullet.

Here's Tammy and her lazy cat, Kipper.

And this is Trig. She has a parrot called Gulliver.

The three little pirates live aboard their ship, the *Lucky Lobster*.

It has:

a **wheel** for steering

a **deck**

a **gangplank** to walk on

a **galley** where the little pirates cook and eat

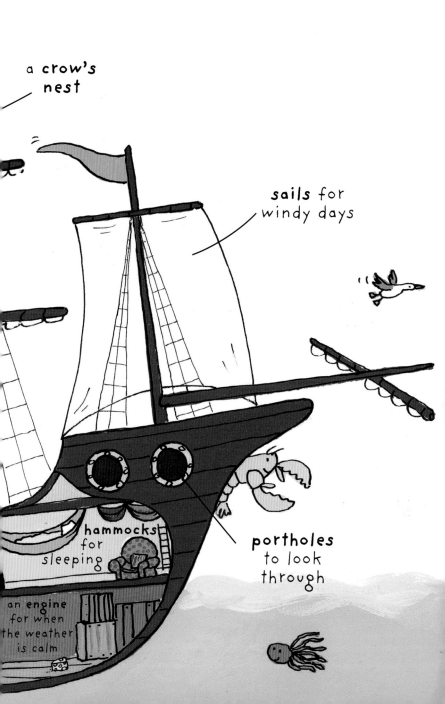

a crow's nest

sails for windy days

hammocks for sleeping

portholes to look through

an engine for when the weather is calm

The three little pirates spend their
days looking for hidden treasure,

keeping the *Lucky Lobster* ship-shape,

and going to Miss Peggy Leggy's
Pirate School for Good (and
sometimes not-so-good)
Little Pirates.

She teaches her pupils
to fire a cannon...

read treasure maps ...

and sing sea songs!

And sometimes the little pirates just like playing with their pirate friends, Toofy and Smudge.

So, now you've met everyone . . .

LET'S GET ON WITH THE STORY!

Chapter 2

A Monster, a Mermaid and a Message

One morning Trixy, Tammy and Trig were asleep in their hammocks when . . .

BOOM! BOOM! WHOOOSH!

. . . an enormous wave crashed into the *Lucky Lobster*.

The little pirates woke with a start.
'Limping lugworms!' said Trixy.
'Jumping jellyfish!' said Tammy.
Trig was under her duvet. She had fallen on the floor!

Trixy, Tammy and Trig had just enough
time to get dressed before . . .

BOOM! WHOOOSH!

A second wave struck the *Lucky Lobster*.
The little pirates raced up on deck to see
what was going on. And then they heard
a very loud . . .

HICCUP.

The hiccup was quickly followed by a *BOOM!* and a *WHOOOSH!* as another wave crashed into them.

Suddenly Trig pointed straight ahead. 'THERE!' she yelled.

The little pirates found themselves staring at their friend, Errol the sea monster.

'Sorry about the hiccups. Too much fizzy seaweed pop!' boomed Errol. And another hiccup rumbled from his tummy.

Suddenly Tammy remembered a way to stop hiccups.

'Hold your breath and count to ten,' she said.

So Errol took a deep breath IN and the little pirates slowly counted to ten.

Errol's cheeks puffed up like pink balloons.
'Four . . . five . . .'

His eyes rolled.
'Six . . . seven. . .'

His cheeks turned red.
'Eight . . . nine . . .'

Bright red.
'TEN!'

Then Errol, bursting for air,
breathed out . . .

PHEWOOOOOOOOOOOOOO!

. . . and blew everyone
off their feet!

There was silence.

Errol's hiccups had stopped.

'Thank you, little pirates!' said Errol.
'I've got an important message for you.'

He took out a white pebble, as shiny as
the moon.

Suddenly the pebble made a loud
ringing noise.

Peep-peep-dooodley-pip-pip-pip!

The pebble was a magic moonstone!

At first, all the little pirates could see was a cloud of mist. When the mist cleared, there, staring out at them was . . .

a MERMAID!

'My name is Mo,' said the mermaid. 'I need your help. There's a pirate called Vanilla Cringe . . .'

The little pirates gasped. Vanilla Cringe was the meanest, greediest pirate-lady who had ever sailed the Salty Sea.

Trixy, Tammy and Trig remembered some of the villainous things she had done.

Mo went on. 'Vanilla's caught my mermates and sold them to a horrid collector! Please, please ... do something!'

'Keep the moonstone safe!' Mo said. Then she was gone, and Errol swam away.

The little pirates stared at one another. They had to help Mo and her friends. It was the most important thing they had ever been asked to do.

Chapter 3
Mo and the Magic Moonstone

Hi! I'm Mo. Here's a bit more about me and how I came to ask the three little pirates for their help!

Mo lived in the Coral Palace with her father, King Codswallop, and her mother, Queen Pearl.

The king and queen tried to give the mermaid princess everything she wanted. But for an adventurous mermaid like Mo, life at the palace was a little bit dull.

Whenever she could, Mo would sneak past the soldier-crab guards to play around Dolphin Island with her friends.

Little did she know that the wicked pirate, Vanilla Cringe, had been keeping an eye on Mo and her fishy friends for some time. She was waiting for the right moment.

One night Vanilla spotted Mo and all
her friends, playing in the moonlight.
She ordered her crew of sea dogs, Gripe,
Muzzle and Boots, to capture them.

'HELP! H-H-H-HELP!' cried the terrified
mermaids and merboys, struggling in the nets.

Mo watched as her friends were slung aboard Vanilla's ship, the *Slinky Shark*, and locked in a cage.

Vanilla praised her crew. 'Well done, my beauties!' Then she added, 'I trust you got them ALL?'

We may p-p-possibly, just possibly, have m-m-missed one.

J-j-just the one.

Mo overheard Vanilla shout: 'You blockheads! You've let the prize one get away. She's the princess mermaid. She's worth a fortune! We must catch her later. Come on. Let's take the others to sell to the collector.'

Mo had no idea what she meant. Who was the collector? And what now? What *could* she do?

Just then, her best friend, Errol the sea monster, came along.

Errol listened as Mo told him the whole story. He could see the *Slinky Shark* heading out to sea.

Errol and Mo followed Vanilla's ship
until, at last, the *Slinky Shark* dropped anchor.

They watched as the cage holding
its fishy load was lowered over the side.
Mo dived after it, but what she
saw next made her gasp . . .

Deep down in the murky depths was an enormous glass palace. The doors and windows were barred with bones. Suddenly, a giant octopus appeared! Mo looked on in horror as the octopus unlocked the cage and pushed her mermates through the door.

Vanilla has done well. But, let me see, there's one more. Princess Mo. The most valuable one of all!

Just then, Errol swam down beside Mo. 'I'd know that scary monster anywhere. That's Hong Kong the octopus. He collects ... things,' he whispered.

They watched Hong Kong struggling to the surface, carrying a heavy bag on each arm.

'And there's much more ... when you bring me the princess,' said Hong Kong.

'I think we should ... GO!' said Errol quickly.

GOLD!

As they hurried away, Mo's head was spinning. They had to rescue everyone from that horrid place. But how?

'I know three little pirates who might help,' said Errol.

'Really?' said Mo. 'Could you give them a message?'

burp! hic! hic! phewooo!

She took from her bag the magic moonstone she had been given by a beautiful witch called Sophie.

Mo thought really, really hard. Could she get a message to the little pirates through the moonstone?

Then she handed Errol the moonstone, and he set off to look for the little pirates.

That morning, as Mo made her way home
. . . *she was caught!*

'It's off to the collector for you!' cried
Vanilla, cackling with delight.

Locked in the cage, Mo screwed her eyes
up tight, willing the moonstone to work
again. Oh, *please*, little pirates, she thought,
thinking as hard as she could.

I NEED YOUR HELP RIGHT NOW!

Chapter 4

A Surprise Meeting with Vanilla

Back aboard the *Lucky Lobster*, the little pirates sped towards Dolphin Island.

As Tammy looked through her telescope, she saw a ship heading their way.

'It's the *Slinky Shark*,' she cried. 'It belongs to Vanilla!'

Suddenly, they saw Vanilla Cringe appear
on the deck. She looked a terrifying sight.

The *Slinky Shark* was coming towards them fast. Just in time Trixy spun the wheel and avoided a crash. The *Slinky Shark* went by with a WHOOOSH!

Out of my way, you drippy little pirates!

Vanilla shouted at her crew. 'Faster, you mangy mongrels!'

The sea-dogs, Gripe, Muzzle and Boots, quickly hoisted another sail, to make the ship go faster and the *Slinky Shark* sped away.

But the little pirates didn't know how soon they were to meet Vanilla again!

Chapter 5

Dolphin Island

Now the little pirates were more determined than ever to find Mo and rescue her mermates.

Soon the *Lucky Lobster* arrived at the harbour on Dolphin Island.

Trixy, Tammy and Trig hoped their friends, Toofy and Smudge, might help them.

They found the pirate boys busy by the river.

'Hi!' said Toofy.

'Great to see you!' said Smudge.

'What *are* you doing?' asked Tammy.

'It's my invention,' Smudge said proudly. 'We're making a . . . submarine! Brilliant, eh? We'll be the first underwater pirates ever!'

WHACK!

'Yeah,' said Toofy. 'It'll be really COOL!'

'Aha!' said Trixy, suddenly very interested in Smudge's invention. 'Now a submarine could come in handy . . .'

'We'll help you get 'em!' said Toofy after Trixy had explained about Mo and her mermates.

'You bet!' said Smudge.

Trixy, Tammy and Trig looked in dismay at the mass of broken timbers and pots of paint on the riverbank.

'Er, when will it be ready?' Trig asked.

'Can't say exactly,' said Smudge. 'Submarines can be tricky.'

'Maybe we could help?' said Tammy.

Trixy, Tammy and Trig had great fun
helping Toofy and Smudge with the
submarine. It was taking shape FAST.

'Thanks for your help,' said the boys.

'See you later!' shouted Trixy, Tammy and Trig.

Then the little pirates hurried to see Mr Spoons at the Harbour Stores.

'We'll need food, a map of the island and stuff like that,' said Trixy.

'And a book about mermaids, and where to find them,' Tammy said.

And Jolly Polly parrot seed!

Mr Spoons was very pleased to see them.
'Can I help you?' he said.

Can YOU find all the things on the pirates' shopping list?

A packet of prawnflakes,
a notebook and pencil,
Meaty Matey, Purrkins,
Jolly Polly seed . . .

. . . and mermaids. We need
a book about mermaids.

'Aah,' said Mr Spoons. 'Mermaids!
I believe they're an endangered species?'

'Yes,' said Tammy. 'We happen to know
some who are.' And she told Mr Spoons all
they knew about Mo.

Dead-eyed dogfish!
I read something
about a mermaid in the
Dolphin Times. It's
around here
somewhere . . .

DOLPHIN
ISLAND

SWIMMING
RESULTS

IT'S A
GAME
OF TWO HALVES

THE DOLPHIN TIMES

A FISHY
BUSINESS

LATE
NEWS
EXTRA!

A coastguard
reported seeing
a mermaid in
distress around
the Quicksand Bay area.
Pirates with large fishing nets
were spotted acting suspiciously.

TREASURE
MAP

'Fishhooks!' exclaimed Trixy. 'That could be Mo! And those suspicious pirates . . .'

'Vanilla and her crew!' said Mr Spoons. 'Do you think they've caught Mo already?'

'I've a horrible feeling you're right,' said Trig. 'Do you know anyone who could help us find her?'

Mr Spoons thought for a moment, then he said, 'Go and see Sophie. She lives at Quicksand Bay. Sophie can't speak but she has . . . *special powers.*'

The little pirates paid for their shopping, then walked back to the *Lucky Lobster*.

And at that very moment, the moonstone in Trixy's pocket went . . .

Peep-peep-dooodley-pip-pip-pip!

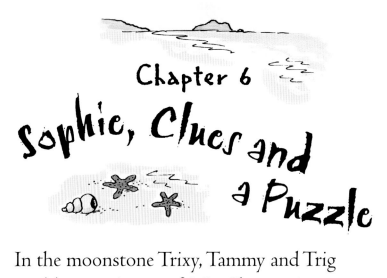

Chapter 6
Sophie, Clues and a Puzzle

In the moonstone Trixy, Tammy and Trig could see a picture of Mo. She was in a cage.

'Oh, no!' wailed Trixy.

'Where are you?' cried Tammy.

H-E-L-P!

Mo's voice was the tiniest whisper.

Before Mo could explain, the moonstone faded. Once again, it looked like a pebble.

'We must go and see Sophie,' said Trixy. 'Mr Spoons said she might help.'

The little pirates looked at the map of Dolphin Island. They soon found Quicksand Bay where Sophie lived.

So the little pirates set off. Near the rope bridge they saw Toofy and Smudge, finishing their submarine.

'Good luck!' cried the three little pirates as they hurried over the bridge.

The little pirates walked along the cliffs to Quicksand Bay. They clambered down a rocky path to the beach and ran along the sand looking for Sophie.

Trixy pointed to a little wooden hut. It was painted blue and decorated with pebbles and shells.

Out of nowhere, a beautiful girl appeared. She had long golden hair and wore a necklace of seashells. It was Sophie.

Sophie seemed to know exactly why the little pirates had come. She took them to a magic pool, then knelt down and gazed silently into the water.

After a while, Sophie stood up and drew some pictures in the sand.

Sophie nodded.

'Flipping flatfish! The tide is coming in!' cried Trixy. 'Quick, Trig! Copy the pictures in your notebook. We'll work them out later.'

Before the little pirates left, Sophie gave them each a necklace of seashells.

After the little pirates had gone, Sophie played a tune on her reed-pipe, and then three friendly dolphins swam off to deliver a very important message to King Codswallop and Queen Pearl.

On board the *Lucky Lobster* the little pirates looked at the clues in Trig's notebook.

'A key,' said Trixy, pointing to the first one.

'To a door . . . in a cage!' said Tammy.

'Right,' said Trig. 'And the shark has to be the *Slinky Shark*. Mo's in a cage, on board the *Slinky Shark*.'

'What about the octopus?' said Trixy.

'Maybe he's . . . the collector?' suggested Tammy.

They all looked at the last clue.

'A bald head,' said Trig. 'What does *that* mean?'

Trixy grabbed the map of Dolphin Island. 'Look!' she said. '*Bald Head.* It's on the map. Vanilla is making for Bald Head!'

YO-HO-
HO!

Let's GO-
GO-GO!

and
CATCH
HER!

Chapter 7

A Race Against Time!

Now the little pirates knew where Vanilla was headed, there was no time to lose. Tammy scrambled up to the crow's nest. To her dismay, she saw black clouds out at sea. Then they all heard a rumble of thunder.

Looks like we're in for a storm!

'Hoist the mainsail!' cried Trixy. 'Let's go!'

Just then the pirate boys came along in their submarine.

Close behind was Errol the sea monster. He had been drinking more seaweed pop.

'Follow us!' shouted Trig. 'You, too, Errol!'

The storm was gathering force, and soon the *Lucky Lobster* was battling through heavy seas and rain.

Suddenly Tammy gave a shout: '*Slinky Shark* ahead!'

The chase was on!

Aboard the *Slinky Shark*, Vanilla was screaming orders at the sea dogs. The ship pitched and rolled. Thunder boomed.

And nearby, tossed around in a cage, was Mo! She clung to the bars as the cage slid from one side of the deck to the other.

The *Lucky Lobster* was catching up with Vanilla, and soon Trig spotted Mo.

'There she is!' she cried.

At that moment, Errol, who had been rolling about in the waves, gave an enormous . . . HICCUP!

A wave as big as a mountain crashed into the *Slinky Shark*. It sent Mo's cage skidding across the deck . . . and INTO THE SEA.

BOOM! WHOOoSH!

SPLASH!

Vanilla was furious. 'Get her back!' she yelled at her crew. But neither Gripe, Muzzle nor Boots could swim!

'We must get Mo out!' shouted Tammy.

Tammy and Trig dived overboard, while Trixy steered the ship. They were wearing Sophie's necklaces. As they swam deeper and deeper, the little pirates found they could swim better than ever, and even BREATHE underwater too.

We can swim like fish with these necklaces!

Suddenly they saw two huge yellow eyes coming towards them. It was Toofy and Smudge in their submarine! The headlights shone through the murky water, and picked out something on the seabed.

In a flash, Tammy and Trig zoomed to open the door.

'I knew you'd come,' said Mo.

But just as the little pirates and Mo were safely back on board the *Lucky Lobster*, Trixy spotted the *Slinky Shark*. Now Vanilla was chasing them!

'We've got to rescue your friends. Let's go!' said Trixy.

Would the little pirates get to the collector's place before Vanilla caught up with them?

Chapter 8
Smash, Grab and a Battle!

Vanilla Cringe scowled. She could see the *Lucky Lobster* ahead.

'I'll get Mo back somehow!' she muttered.

When the two ships were close enough, Vanilla grabbed a rope, made a lasso and let it fly. *Swish!*

'GOTCHA!' Vanilla cried as she caught Mo.

'Don't worry about me,' Mo called to the little pirates. 'Rescue my friends first.'

Down, down, down. Trixy, Tammy and Trig swam, as fast as fishes, to the bottom of the sea. Toofy and Smudge dived in their submarine. And there, straight ahead, was the palace! It was huge and Mo's friends were trapped inside.

SWOOOSH!

Two fierce swordfish swam by.

'Guards!' wailed Trig. 'Now we're for it!'
The guards headed straight for the little
pirates, but before they could attack, Toofy
and Smudge took the swordfish by surprise.

There was an earsplitting CRASH! as the submarine smashed through the bars, and seconds later, everyone swam out.

We're free!

WOWEEE!

Hong Kong lunged at the escaping mermaids and merboys. It was a great battle! But one by one, Mo's friends swam to safety. Then Trixy, Tammy and Trig helped the pirate boys out of their submarine.

Meanwhile, Vanilla dangled Mo over the side of her ship, waiting for Hong Kong. Suddenly, out of the sea, came HUNDREDS of soldier crabs! They marched on to the ship, with their sword-sharp pincers.

OW! OW! OW!

Thanks to Sophie's message, King Codswallop had sent his army to help!

'Wicked!' cried Mo, escaping Vanilla's clutches. With a flick of her tail, she swam back to the *Lucky Lobster*.

Everyone on board cheered!

Vanilla knew when she was beaten.

It was the last anyone saw of Vanilla and her crew.

Meanwhile Hong Kong had given up mermaid-collecting. He went back to his lair and was never heard of again.

Chapter 9
A Party for the Pirates!

The moon shone bright and clear as the
Lucky Lobster drifted into the harbour.

Trixy, Tammy and Trig were greeted with
shouts and cheers.

The news of their battle had flashed round Dolphin Island like lightning.

As they came ashore, they heard a fanfare of trumpets. *Tan-tan-terrah!*

'It's my mum and dad!' cried Mo.

Sure enough, King Codswallop and Queen Pearl had just arrived in a splendid sea-carriage.

The king thanked the little pirates for rescuing his daughter and all her friends, and Queen Pearl presented the awards.

There were gold medals for Trixy, Tammy and Trig for being Very Brave Little Pirates, a box of treasure for Toofy and Smudge, and an extra-large bottle of seaweed pop for Errol.

Suddenly there was a terrific BANG!
followed by a fizzing Z-Z-Z-Z-OOOOOM!
Then a million stars burst into the sky.

Everyone had a wonderful time.

When, at last, it was time for them all to go to bed, three sleepy little pirates climbed into their hammocks.

'Goodnight, Trixy.'   'Goodnight, Tammy.'   'Goodnight, Trig.'

Goodnight, little pirates.
Goodnight!

Look out for

The Three Little Princesses

Tan-tan-terrah!

Meet Phoebe, Pruella and Pip.

It's the king's birthday but everything
will go wrong unless the three little
princesses can find the missing
key to the magic clock.

£4.99

978 1 84255 633 7